Chris Denroche

A Souvenir History of the Parish of Saint Paul's

Kent County, Maryland

Chris Denroche

A Souvenir History of the Parish of Saint Paul's
Kent County, Maryland

ISBN/EAN: 9783337429492

Printed in Europe, USA, Canada, Australia, Japan

Cover: Foto ©Andreas Hilbeck / pixelio.de

More available books at **www.hansebooks.com**

A Souvenir History

— OF THE —

PARISH OF ST. PAUL'S,

Kent County, Maryland.

COMPILED FOR THE

Bi-Centennial Celebration

— OF ITS —

FOUNDATION IN 1693,

— BY —

THE REV. CHRIS. T. DENROCHE,

— RECTOR OF —

St. Paul's Church and of Christ Church, I. U. District,

KENT COUNTY, MARYLAND, IN 1893.

OLD S. PAUL'S CHURCH, KENT CO., MD.,

AS IT STANDS IN 1893.

Building Commenced August, 1711.   Finished February, 1713.

A Souvenir History

—OF THE—

PARISH OF ST. PAUL'S,

Kent County, Maryland.

COMPILED FOR THE

Bi-Centennial Celebration

OF ITS —

FOUNDATION IN 1693,

— BY—

THE REV. CHRIS. T. DENROCHE,

—RECTOR OF—

St. Paul's Church and of Christ Church, I. U. District,

KENT COUNTY, MARYLAND, IN 1893.

Entered according to Act of Congress, in the year 1893, by CHRIS. T. DENROCHE, in the office of the Librarian of Congress, at Washington, D. C.

Chestertown Transcript Steam Book Print.

SECTION I.

NEW YARMOUTH TOWN.

TAKEN from a diary said to have been written in about 1773, by Peregrine Wroth, Esq , there was an account of the town of New Yarmouth, not long ago submitted in extracts to our local press.

These extracts contain also all the evidence I can find of a church building on Eastern Neck, previous to the foundation of St. Paul's Parish in sixteen hundred and ninety three. It is as follows, (in substance) :

The town of New Yarmouth was built upon land purchased of Major Thomas Ringgold, by a man named Tovey.

Tovey bought 100 acres out of a tract of land called Huntingfield, which is stretched across and to the south of Eastern Neck.

In 1838 the farms of that tract belonged to George W. Willson, Esq., and others.

The writer of the extracts and George L. Davis, Esq., visited this locality and found the remains of a wharf, covered with rubbish, and also many stones which were not native to Maryland, but which had been brought in ships, as ballast, from England ; said ships returned to England having tobacco as chief cargo. The stones had been used to pave the approach to the wharves, and for other purposes.

In 1838 Thomas Browne owned this land.

New Yarmouth was, in its day, a commercial centre, and a port of customs entry : the court sat there, and there the King's justices met.

Bye and bye, as this commercial centre became inconvenient, a new town was built seven or eight miles down the river, and this too, proving inconvenient, a new town was started where Chestertown now stands.

The Rev. Dr. Robert Willson, in Lippincott's Magazine of October, 1876, says that New Yarmouth was founded by James Ringgold about 1680 ; and that by statute it was made a port of entry in 1684. He states, also, that a creek near by, called Church Creek, was so called, doubtless, from the site of a house of worship which once stood there, erected by the colonists.

Major Hanson, in his book "Old Kent," has produced from legal records a note that a court met at New Yarmouth in 1686 ; and another, that legal statute made it a port of entry in 1684.

NEW YARMOUTH CHURCH.

The first church we have any evidence of would appear to have been built in this locality in, or before, 1680 ; possibly previous to the foundation of New Yarmouth town.

Mr. George W. Willson, in 1835, informed the writer of the extracts that an old negro, Nathan Laddy, who died at the age of 100 years, had told him that he remembered when a church stood on his (Mr. Willson's farm.) The writer of the extracts then (in 1838) had excavations made, and found a number of graves, some of which were arched up with brick. Mr. Willson testified also that there were many English bricks scattered about the place. The first cargo of bricks from England came in 1666.

Kent county was settled from Eastern Neck Island, and settlements were made towards the north of the county. This accounts for a church being built north of the Island.

There is now, in 1893, on a farm called Hermitage, owned by Mrs. Hallie Brown, widow of the late Dr. Thos. R. Brown, tenanted by Mr John Brice, Jr., and situated on the east side of the main Eastern Neck road, a mound, surmounted by trees, which is pointed out as the first church and cemetery site of the old time. This mound is now called Old St. Paul's graveyard.

In a short time, and to meet the convenience of the northern trend of the settlers, and when the Parish of St. Paul's was founded by law, the church site was moved from this New Yarmouth locality to the place it now occupies, at the head of Broad nox Creek.*

SECTION II.

FOUNDATION OF THE PARISH OF ST. PAUL'S.

From Hanson's " Old Kent," Page 322.

"At their majesties' court, holden for Kent county, the 28th day of November, in the fifth year of their Majesties' reign, 1693, (there were present) Capt. Hans Hanson, Mr. Edward Sweetman, Mr. Dan Norris, Mr. John Copedge, Justices." It was "ordered by the court that the 19th of this instant, December, be ye day for electing ye Vestrymen at ye Town of New Yarmouth."

"At a court, holden by their Majesties' Justices for Kent county, at the Town of New Yarmouth, for laying out ye upper part of this county into parishes, this 19th day of December, in ye 5th year of their Majesties' (William and Mary) reign. Annoq. Dom., 1693."

The Justices, with the advice of the most principal freeholders present, doe lay out ye upper part of this county for one District or Parish, by ye name

*For the use of the term " Broad nox " see entry on Appendix E—March 15, 1841—" Horatio Beck, Broad Knox."

of St. Peter's, (now St. Paul's,) to begin at ye lower end of Eastern Neck, bounded by Chester river and ye bay, so far as ye plantation that formerly did belong to Plarness, and from thence by ye division line between Kent and Cecil county.

Entered pr. Charles Bass, Clk : "Their majesties do appoint ye 20th day of January for electing Vestrymen at the Town of New Yarmouth."

"January the 24th, 1693-4, being the day appointed, according to a former order of the Justices of this county, for the electing and chusing of Vestrymen for St. Peter's Parish, on which day, at a meeting of ye most principal Freeholders and Justices, as aforesaid, at ye house of Mr. Thomas Smith, at ye Towne of New Yarmouth, doth by a free election elect six Vestrymen : Mr. Thomas Smith,* Mr. William Frisby, Mr. Charles Tilden, Mr. Mich. Miller, Mr. Hans Hanson, Mr Simon Wilmer."

FROM OLD RECORD BOOKS OF ST. PAUL'S CHURCH.

Pursuant to an Act of Assembly, entituled an act for the service of Almighty God and the establishment of the Protestant religion of this Province, wherein it is ordered that the counties within the Province of Maryland shall be divided into Parishes, and likewise it is ordered by the same law that the Justices of the county, with the freeholders of the county, shall chuse six Vestrymen for each respective Parish, which accordingly was done and performed on the 24th day of January, Anno qui Domini, 1693, whose names are hereunder inserted, vizt :

Jan. 30, 1693.	Mr. Thomas Smith,	Mr. Charles Tilden,
	Mr. William Frisby,	Mr. Michael Miller,
	Mr. Hans Hanson,	Mr. Simon Wilmer.

FIRST VESTRY MEETING OF ST. PAUL'S PARISH.

The first vestry meeting of St. Paul's Parish was held in the house of Mr. Thomas Joce, of New Yarmouth, on or immediately after 30th Jany., 1693.

The early vestry meetings were held in the houses of Mr. Michael Miller, of Langford's Bay, Mr. Thomas Joce, of New Yarmouth, and of Mr. Simon Wilmer.

CHURCH BUILDING.

FIRST PROPOSAL FOR BUILDING A CHURCH IN THE PRESENT LOCALITY, BUT NOT CARRIED OUT.

By a meeting of the Vestry at the house of Mr. Thomas Joce, for the Parish of St. Paul's, on the north side Chester river. Agreed about the dimensions of a church to be built upon part of a tract of land belonging to Mr. Michael Miller, which is called the main branch of Broad nox Creek, vizt : Fifty feet long, etc., wherein Mr. Norris was desired to consider of and report the charge to the vestry the fifteenth day of February next. (1693).

*Note.—Thomas Smith is entered as "Smith" up to 5th September, 1691; after that date his name is recorded as "Smyth."

A full attendance of Vestry met on the fifteenth day of February, 1693; chose Mr. Michael Miller and William Frisby principals. Mr. Norris did there and then deliver the account of his charges, which charges the vestry decided were too large, and did not accept. The Vestry then agreed with Mr. Norris for making one hundred and thirty thousand bricks, and fifteen hundred tile of ten inches square and two inches thick.

Mr. Norris was ordered on July 24th, 1693, not to make the bricks.

SECOND PROPOSAL FOR BUILDING A CHURCH, BUT NOT CARRIED OUT.

The Vestry met at Mr. Michael Miller's house on 29th January, 1694. A proposal was made to Mr. Daniel Norris to take a contract to build a church. Mr. Norris to give charges on 14th February, 1694.

Proposed plan of church was 52 feet long and 26 feet wide, outside to outside. The foundation to be raised with brick three feet above the ground, and upon the brick to be framed with good substantial timber eleven foot pitch above the brick. The posts to stand ten foot asunder, with the girders and five principal rafters, and other timber to be proportionable to such a building; five windows six feet wide, the height proportionable, with shutters to the same: a pair of folding door. in the front.

THIRD PROPOSAL FOR BUILDING A CHURCH.

This proposal was carried out, and the church was built: but it was erected before the present church building.

On April 15th, 1695, the vestry met at the house of Mr. Thomas Joce, at New Yarmouth, and agreed with Mr. Daniel Norris to build a church 40 feet long and 24 feet wide, Foundation to be raised with brick three feet above the ground, and a substantial timber building to be erected on this foundation; ten feet pitch above the brick; posts ten feet asunder; five girders and five principal rafters, and other timber proportionable; three windows six foot wide, and height proportionable, with folding doors to the same; a pair of folding doors in the front; a ten-foot chancel, to be paved with Tile; a six foot Ile the length of the church, to be paved with tile. This in consideration of twenty-one thousand pounds of tobacco, whereof there is paid the sum of fifteen thousand pounds two hundred and ninety-nine.

Mr. Daniel Norris entered into this contract and gave bond in 42,000 pounds of every way good tobacco. The work was to be completed at or before the last day of November, 1695, or bond to be forfeited.

The Vestry then gave Mr. Daniel Norris an order on Sheriff Tilden for 5,249 pounds of tobacco, being the full amount remaining in the Sheriff's hands, due to the Parish of St. Paul's, and took Mr. Norris' receipt for the 15,299 pounds already paid to him.

DESCRIPTION OF THE CHURCH LOT.

Date, 6th Feby., 1696. The church was built upon a parcel of land belonging to Michael Miller, being part of a tract of land called Arcadia, lying at the head of Broad nox Creek, bounding on the south with a parcel of land called The Fork, formerly laid out for Henry Hawkins ; and on the north with a parcel of land formerly laid out for James Ringgold ; and on the west by John Wadd's land. The Vestry have agreed with the said Michael Miller to give him two thousand pounds of tobacco for the aforesaid land, and the said Michael Miller will oblige himself to make over the said land at March court next.

Some seeming difficulty exists in the records as to the locality of Michael Miller's lands. The record of 6th February, 1696, shows that the church "was built on M. Miller's land, which was part of a tract called Arcadia, at the *head of Broad nox Creek.*" The record of June 6th, 1696, shows that a "meeting of the vestry was held at M. Miller's plantation, *on Langford's Bay.*" But, by an entry of February 6th, 1696, the record shows a "vestry meeting at Michael Miller's old plantation." The difficulty will be solved if we find that Michael Miller had two plantations—a new and an old one ; one on Langford's Bay and one at the head of Broad nox Creek.

I cannot make out, though, as to the identical site of the first St. Paul's Church ; for, continuing to examine the Records, I find an entry of 27th Nov., 1707, as follows : "Ordered by this Vestry that Charles Ringgold be paid two thousand pounds of Tobacco for what timber was cut off his land and used in building the church, and five hundred pounds of Tobacco for two acres of land that the church is built on, by order of a Jury." Hence there was a church built previous to 27th Nov., 1707, on two acres of land owned and sold by Charles Ringgold.

CHARLES RINGGOLD'S LOT.

But note further that the Records show an entry of 11th Nov., 1699, as follows : "We, the undersigned, being summoned and sworn to value two acres of land, *adjacent to the Parish Church of St. Paul's Parish,* on the north side Chester, and now run out by the Vestry of said Parish, we do value the said two acres of land at five hundred pounds of tobacco."

TWO CHURCHES.

It would appear, then, that in 1707 there were two buildings or churches, one, built as a Parish Church of St. Paul's, on "Michael Miller's land"; the other built "adjacent to the Parish Church of St. Paul's," on two acres bought from Charles Ringgold.*

But of the church before mentioned as having been built by Mr. Daniel Norris, it was not finished according to contract ; for the Vestry sued Mr. Daniel Norris for his unfulfilled contract, and on Nov. 27th, 1707, obtained judgment against him for 4,673 lbs. tobacco and 299 lbs. for costs of suit, though he (Mr. Daniel Norris) gave a receipt on 6th Feb., 1696, in full for payment for building the church.

---

*C. Ringgold got 500 lbs. Tobacco for his two acres ; M. Miller got 2,000 lbs. Tobacco for his lot ; at that rate M. Miller's land, which was bought for a church lot, would have been 8 acres.

On March 1st, 1696, Robert Norris and Richard Scrivener agree to pail in a church-yard 100 feet square, to recover said church, to rail in a chancel, to build a pulpit and reading pew for 4,500 lbs. of tobacco; work to be finished by last of August, 1696.

On July 24th, 1697, the vestry contracted with Mr. Robert Norris to arch the church fit for plaistering from the plate to the windbeam, to put in a six foot wainscot with moulding, to lay the ground sills, to seat the chancel and to make a communion table 6 ft. x 3ft., for 4,500 lbs. of tobacco. Work to be finished by the last day of October, 1697.

On 27th Jan'y, 1697, Robert Norris agreed to build thirteen pews and a gallery, for 12,000 lbs. of tobacco.

On 13th May, 1698, Gideon Gamble, of Cecil county, contracted to plaister the church for 3,500 lbs. of tobacco. The vestry to find him in nails and hair.

John Salter glaized the windows 24th Feb'y, 1699.

On Sep 14, 1700, the brick work of the church is reported as decaying. It was taken down in April 25th, 1702, and replaced with stone.

THOMAS SMYTH'S SILVER COMMUNION VESSELS.

On April 9th, 1699, Major Thomas Smyth doth present to the Parish of St Paul's, on the north side of Chester river, as a gift, one Challice of Silver and one Plate of Silver, engraved on them as followeth, vizt :

The gift of to the Parish of St. Paul's, on the north side Chester.

A chalice of silver, worth about $70.00, and exactly like to the chalice of silver presented to the church by Thomas Smyth in 1699, was presented to St. Paul's at the instigation of Judge Chambers, after the last visitation of Bishop Whittingham, between 1861 and 1864. Judge Chambers paid one-half of its cost, and the ladies of the congregation raised the balance. It bears the inscription : "Gift of the ladies of the congregation to St. Paul's Church, on the north side Chester.

ELINER SMYTH'S PRESENTATION.

August 3rd, 1703, Eliner Smyth, wife of Thomas Smyth, this day was pleased to present the church with a pulpit cloth and a cushion, with this motto or inscription in the pulpit cloth :

S
I H
The Gift of E. S.
To St. Paul's Church,
North Side Chester River,
1703.

REV. ALEX. WILLIAMSON'S APPOINTMENT.

May 10, 1711, Rev. Mr. Alexander Williamson, being an Orthodox minister of the Church of England, sent certified and Recommended by the Right Honorable and Reverend Father in God, Henry, Lord Bishop of London, to Officiate within this Province. You are hereby required to Receive him as Rector of your Parish, to which he is hereby appointed and presented.

Given at the Council Chamber, at the City of Annapolis, the Fourteenth Day of April, in the Tenth year of the Reign of our Sovereign Lady, Queen Ann, of Great Britain. Anno qui Domini, 1711.

Edw'd Lloyd.   [Seal].

WILLIAM PEARLE'S GIFT OF LAND.

On July 10th, 1711, the vestry appointed Mr. James Harris to run out that land which was given by Wm. Pearle for the use and benefit of the poor of this parish, lying in Langford's Bay, called Spencix.

This land was rented to Capt. Scott on March 18, 1711, for 7 years, at 300 lbs. tobacco per annum.

SECTION III.

THE PRESENT CHURCH BUILDING, NOW STANDING.

At a meeting of the Vestry at the Parish Church of St. Paul's, in Kent county, August 27, 1711 : (Rev'd) Mr. Alex. Williamson, Mr. Wm. Scott, Capt. Edw'd Scott, Mr. Wm. Harris, Capt. Jas. Harris, Mr. Wm. Frisby, Sen'r.

This Vestry doth agree with Mr. James Harris, as undertaker, to build a church for the use of this Parish of St. Paul's, in Kent county, according to the Dimensions, following, vizt :

40 feet long in the clear and 30 feet wide in the clear ; to be 16 feet from the ground ; 5 windows, 2 doors and cases ; the brick wall to be 2½ bricks thick to the water-table and 2 bricks thick from thence upwards : A circle to be at the east end for the Communion. The windows and doors and cornish and other work to be proportionable and suitable to such a building, and in Consideration this Vestry doth agree to pay Mr. James Harris seventy thousand pounds of Tobacco.

Geo. Worsley, Cl'k of Vestry.

In addition to above, there was a condition to well shingle the aforesaid house with good cypress shingles, and to be good shutters for all the said house, and the arch in the roof of said house to be finished workmanlike. The work to be finished at or before the tenth day of October, in the year of our Lord Christ one thousand seven hundred and thirteen ; And when so built the afs'd house to be delivered to (Rev'd) Mr. Alex. Williamson, Col. Thomas Smyth, Mr. Wm. Frisby, Mr. Wm. Harris, Mr. Wm. Scott, Edward Scott, to them or either of them, their heirs or either of their heirs, exec'rs, adm'rs, for the only use and Benefit of our said Parish of St. Paul's, in said county.

Mr. James Harris, William Pott and James Smith gave bond to the Vestrymen in one hundred and fifty thousand pounds of good, sound, merchantable leaf Tobacco, and cask to contain the same, for the completion of their contract.

The Vestrymen gave bond to Mr. James Harris for 140,000 pounds of good, sound, merchantable leaf Tobacco, on behalf of St. Paul's Parish, for the due performance of their agreement.

At a meeting of the Vestry on 2nd Feb'y, 1713. This day Capt. James Harris having complied with his obligation to the vestry about building the Church, hath made his delivery of said Church to this vestry and hath taken in his Bond.

Ordered, that notice be given in church and notes set up at the mills about erecting Pews in the church.

Mr. James Harris was allowed 600 lbs. Tobacco, or £2 5s., for extra work above his obligation.*

On 20th Feb'y, 1713-14. The Vestry contracted with William Salisbury, of Queen Anne's county, to erect and set up thirty-four Pews, Pulpits and Reading Desk, according to a model by the said vestry drawn. The Sells to the afs'd work to be of Cedar or Locust. The work to be finished by the ninth day of September ensuing, in consideration of eighteen thousand pounds of Tobacco.

William Salisbury gave legal bond to the vestry in 36,000 pounds of Tobacco for the due completion of his part, and the vestry gave legal bond in 36,000 pounds of Tobacco to William Salisbury for the due completion of their part of the contract.

On 17th March, 1714, Wm. Mackey was to make moulds for the glazier, to put stantions in the Windows and to fit the two Doors with a Lock to one and a Cross Barr on the inside of the other, for 500 lbs. Tobacco.

On May 22, 1714, Capt'n Wm. Pott and Capt'n St. Legia Codd were ordered to employ a plaisterer. Col. Nathaniel Hynson agreed to glaize the windows, and so did.

A tax of 10 lbs. Tobacco on each tax-payer was continually levied each year, pursuant to an Act of Assembly, for Repairing, Beautifying or Building Churches.

On 17th Jan'y, 1714, notice was given in Church and notes set up at the Mills for those who had taken seats to meet the vestry on the 29th Jan'y.

On May 15, 1715, Lieut. Col. Edw'd Scott is sworn vestryman in the room of Col. Thos. Smyth.

On April 10th, 1715, the vestry agreed with Thos. Cook to plaister the church and chancel, to lay the Oils (aisles) and Alter (altar) with brick, at his own charges, the brick to be laid herring-bone fashion and a new joint, to be finished by the last day of August. The vestry obliged themselves to pay said Cook 10,000 lbs. of Tobacco by the first day of May, 1716.

---

*At this rate, Tobacco, (good, sound, merchantable leaf, with cask convenient), was worth (in 1713) about three farthings per pound, English money, or one and three-quarters of a cent, American money (at present rate of exchange in 1883.)

It was ordered by the vestry that Wm. Deane hath leave to pull down the old Church and to have the Nails for his Pains. Note: Wm. Deane did not pull down the Church on those terms.

On 16th May, 1715, the Vestry agreed with Wm. Mackey to Build a Gallery in the new church and to make use of the old stuff in the old church: work to be finished, without hindering the plaisterers, by 20th September, 1715, in consideration of 8,000 pounds of Tobacco.

Thomas Smith is allowed 250 pounds Tobacco for nails and smoothing and nailing the arch peices in the ceiling.

On Feb. 20, 1716, Thomas Cook was sued for failure to complete his contract. Judgment was given against him for 1576 lbs. Tobacco in August, 1716, and execution issued against him for 1576 lbs. Tobacco and costs of suit.

In 1717, 20th Nov'r, the Vestry of St. Paul's Parish met in the court house in Chester Town.

On April 18th, 1720, Zacharias Brown agreed to take down all the timber-work of the old church, to carry it clear off the church-yard and to clear off the church-yard according to the directions marked off by the vestry, for 1200 lbs. of Tobacco. Zacharias Brown agreed also to pale in a church yard, and to make 3 gates and 3 upping blocks.

On June 21, 1721, Wm. Mackey was paid 650 lbs. Tobacco for mending Windows, &c.

On April 14, 1724, the vestry paid out 2138 lbs. Tobacco for land, vizt : To purchase of 2 acres of church land of said Mackey, 1500 lbs. Tobacco ; to cleaning the church and finding 3 hasps and 6 hinges, &c., 638 lbs. Tobacco ; total, 2138. And on same date Robert Street was paid 672 lbs. Tobacco for repairing windows.

THE VESTRY HOUSE.

The Vestry House was built in 1766, for 20,000 lbs. Tobacco. (See Appendix.)

27th October, 1800, the Rev. George Dashiel held services at St. Paul's only every other Sunday ; but what he did, or where he went, on the other Sundays, is not said.

On 27th October, 1800, there occurs the first mention of Dollars, where a necessary 50 Dollars is to be raised to do the repairs of the church that must be done immediately.

2nd Feb'y, 1801, 292 panes of glass purchased for church repairs.

11th May, 1801, Simon Willmer is elected as lay delegate to the convention at Baltimore.

7th June, 1802. The collection of Sunday, the 6th, was to defray the expenses of the Lay Delegate to the State Convention, held at Easton ; the balance to go to the secretary of convention and to purchase a Bible and Prayer Book.

27th May, 1801, William Voss rented the Vestry House for a school house at £3 per annum. Mr. Voss to keep the house in repair and mend at all times any broken windows.

3d May, 1802, Thomas Allison made a similar arrangement.

3d Aug , 1807, Mr. Voss made a similar arrangement.

PROPOSALS TO PULL DOWN THE OLD CHURCH AND BUILD A NEW ONE.

On 3rd Aug., 1801, it was resolved that the collection to pay for repairs on the old church should be suspended, and that subscriptions be put on foot immediately for a new church.

The motion was made by Thomas Hynson, Church Warden.

9th April, 1804. Resolved, that a meeting of the parishioners be called to take into consideration the building of a new church.

4th Feb'y, 1805, the Vestry adjourned until Easter Monday for a further consideration of building a new church or repairing the old one.

15th April, 1805, Easter Monday. No action was taken about the new church ; or, at least, no action is recorded.

I'm afraid that if our predecessors of 1801-2-3-4 and 5 had been rich enough they would have pulled down our dear old Church, and so have destroyed a splendid monument of the first days of our history. Thank God they were not able to build a new one, or otherwise they would have destroyed, to the injury of us, their successors, the building which has so many sweetest associations and is so fondly dear to the heart of every one of us.

March 8th, 1806. The Trustees for repairing the church were ordered to proceed forthwith.

May 20th, 1806. 12 rules of vestry, are recorded, for the purpose of securing order and respect and for the prompt dispatch of business.

March 8th, 1806. Resolved, that the windows of the church, the floor and doors shall be finished before any other repairs be gone into.

In 1812 St. Paul's Church was used as a Barracks for the troops, during some time of the war of that date with England. Capt'n Scott, who was maternal grandfather to Mrs. George Jessop (nee Maria Harris), was quartered there.

The church is said to have been at that time, in the form of a cross. It was so, but there is no written record of it. There is at this date (May 24th, 1893,) a bricked-up archway, both in the north and south side walls, and the records for 1824 mention the payment of a bill for taking down the north wing of the church. (See below).

July 2, 1820, Sunday ; Collections to be made for repairing the roof.

Aug. 18, 1821. Vestry to collect money for repairs to the Church, particularly the windows.

April 8, 1822. Business on repairs.

April 16, 1824. After considering what repairs were necessary, it was thought the best way was to take down the north end of the Church and to build a wall across, as the Church was formerly. W. B. Wilmer, James P.

Gale, Wm. F. Harper, Thomas Miller and B. Scott were appointed as a repair committee to report to the vestry.

1824 : Bills of $242.70 were paid for taking down the north wing of the Church, and plastering and repairing the old Church and putting it in its original form, as ordered by vestry of 16th August, 1824.

16th August, 1824. Downey & Bryan, carpenters, presented their bill for repairs, which was thought extravagant, and was submitted to Thomas Davis and Thomas Vickers, who cut down the bill nearly one-half.

THE CHURCH IN DECLINE.

16th April, 1827, Easter Monday. Vestrymen : Wm. B. Wilmer, Thomas Miller, Thomas B. Hynson, Merritt Miller, James P. Gale, James Brown, John Urie, Horatio Beck.

Church Wardens : Joseph Brown, William Crane.

Register : John Scott.

The above were duly elected by the parishioners.

April 27, 1827. Memorandum entered in Record Book, by Wm. B. Wilmer: "During a number of years, as this book too well evinces, this parish was without any regular ministry ; but from certain periods from this time to the following election (on Easter Monday, 16th March, 1838,) of vestry, the Rector of the Chestertown parish officiated First after Dr. Clowes was the Rev'd Mr. Stone, for whom a collection was made and paid. Then the Rev'd Mr. Jones, for whom also a collection was made and paid, as the accounts at the end of this book will show."

There was no regular clergyman at St. Paul's from about 1827 or 1828 until 1839. Occasional arrangements were made for services by the clergymen of Chestertown.

Rev. Clement F. Jones, D. D., of Chestertown, of which parish he was Rector for 22 years, officiated at St. Paul's very frequently. In 1840, during an engagement as temporary Rector of St. Paul's, he married Leonora Scott to Joseph Harris, who were the parents of the present (1893) Mrs. James H. Gale, Mrs. George Jessop and Mrs. George Beck. Rev. Mr. Stone, of Chestertown, gave services at St. Paul's in 1833, 1834, 1835 and 1836.

There is no record of a vestry meeting, nor was there any vestry meeting held from 16th April, 1827, to 31st March, 1834 ; nor from then to March 16th, 1838. The affairs of the church were in a very bad way during these years. The building became altogether dilapidated and almost unfit for use, till it was restored in 1840 and '41.

March 16, 1838 ; The Vestry and Wardens elected were W. B. Wilmer, Thomas Miller, Thomas B. Hynson, Merritt Miller, John Urie, Horatio Beck, James Brown, James P. Gale, Vestrymen : Joseph Brown, Rasin M. Gale, Wardens ; John Scott, Register. The vestry only met and held over, as the law provided, between April 16, 1827, and March 16, 1838.

October, 1839 : The vestry met and engaged the Rev. John Alberger, who was ill and not able to officiate regularly. He resided for a short time with Mr. James P. Gale, then went on a visit to Buffalo, N. Y., and was unable to return to St. Paul's

November, 1840. Vestry met and engaged the Rev'd Frederick W. Boyd, of Portland, Maine, at $450 a year.

THE CHURCH RESTORED.

March 1st. 1841. The Rev. Mr. Boyd submitted a contract, which had been offered to him for repairing the church. It was not acted on. The vestry were to make known the repairs wanted and to invite contracts. Strong & Stevens got the work, and others.

Aug. 8th, 1841. Moved that a Vestry or Robing Room, to be constructed of wood, be erected in the external angle of the northeast side of the chancel. This is not the present Robing Room, which is built of Brick.

January 24th, 1842. A letter from the Rev'd Mr. Boyd, dated Natchez, Dec'r 27, 1841, resigning as Rector of St. Paul's, on account of continued ill health, was read.

The Vestry resolved that Mr. Boyd's resignation be accepted, acknowledging his great usefulness in reviving a church almost sunk ; their sympathy in his affliction ; they hope his recovery may be earlier than circumstances indicate : the great pleasure they would have in greeting him again : and that should the church be without a pastor their determination to invite him again to the Rectorship.

July 2nd, 1842. On motion of Horatio Beck, it was resolved that the pews be distributed by lot, each subscriber to have his choice of pews according to the number drawn, there being as many numbers as subscribers.

17th April, 1843. Funds were collected to put Shutters to the Windows and to finish the Chancel and drapery to the pulpit.

CONSECRATION OF CHURCH.

26th Nov'r. 1843. The Church being complete and finished in every particular, it was consecrated to the service of Almighty God By the Right Reverend William Rollison Whittingham, Bishop of the Diocese of Maryland.

The Rev'd Thomas B. Flower, Rector : Thomas Miller, Wm. B. Wilmer, James P. Gale, James F. Browne, James Browne, Horatio Beck, Alex. W. Ringgold, Henry W. Carvill, Vestrymen ; J. N. Gordon, Sr., Reg'r ; Thos. Miller, Esq., Delegate to Convention.

Jan. 10. 1845. G. C. Griffith was made Sole Supervisor of the Cemetery. Ordered that no separate enclosure should be made for any grave.

At this time St. Paul's owned a slip of land of an acre, more or less, lying between the main road and Dr. Houston's land, beginning at a Boundary of Houston's land, on the Bellair road, and running on with Houston's land to the Rock Hall road. Said slip of land was appropriated for a Sexton's House.

Nov. 19, 1845. Burials, to persons in limited circumstances, and not regular contributors to the parish, are to be $1.00 each ; and in good circumstances, $5.00 each.

19th Nov., 1845 $50 was voted to Roof the South Side of the Church.

Jan. 29th, 1846. Considerable debate was held on the expediency of Fairs. The majority of the Vestry were less favorable to them, and manifestly opposed to having dinners; limiting themselves to an afternoon in the strawberry season and on the fourth of July.

April 13, 1846. The Vestry rescinded their restrictions on Fairs, as passed at last meeting, but will act as may be deemed by them expedient

June 10, 1846. Resolutions of regret and sympathy were passed on the death of James Frisby Brown. Copies were sent to the family and to the *Kent News*.

1847. A dispute arose with the owner of the land north of the church, who had cut down one of the oak trees, and encroached on the Church property by building an ice-house too far on it; since which the Vestry purchased   acres north of the Church grounds as a site for a Sexton's house.

May 20, 1847. The Rev'd F. W Boyd had offered previously to come back to St. Paul's, and his offer was subsequently accepted, but too late, as Mr. Boyd had accepted another call meanwhile.

April 9th, 1849.   Thomas Miller's death announced.

April 21, 1851.   Jacob T. Freeman's death announced.

July 28, 1852.   Mr. Derrickson was to repair the floor of the Church and put a new roof on the Vestry Room, at $1.50 a day.

Mr. Eben F. Perkins, (County Surveyor), Bill of $3.00; ordered to be paid.

June 16, 1854.   Rev'd Mr. Allen, of Baltimore county, examined the old Parish Books so as to publish a history of the Church in Maryland. He then took them to Chestertown for the use of Dr. Pere. Wroth.

May 3. 1858. $500.00 a year voted for a Rector.

Oct. 21, 1859   The Vestry voted to purchase Mount Pleasant farm, known as the Tilden farm, from R. Hynson, trustee, for $1200.00.

$845.00 were subscribed towards it, right then and there.

May 10, 1861.   Resolved, that the Church be repaired.

Jan'y 8, 1862.   Vestry agreed to pay the Rev'd Andrew Sutton's horse and carriage hire and to increase his salary to $500.

The following is recorded at end of Book of Vestry Records, which opens on July 25, 1800, and closes on Jan'y 8, 1862 :

1861. Sept. 30.	Repairs of Church in 1861.		
	Amount of Bill : (No amount is entered).		
1863. April 10.	Purchase of Harmonium,	$	275 00
	Furniture of Chancel and Font		120 00
1864.	Stained Glass Window		250 00
1865,	Altering ——for Gallery		6 00
" [B'ght in '50.]	Purchase of Glebe, paid in full		1200 00
"	Insurance, 1863 to 1865		17 80
1863.	Fence and Enclosing Cemetery		57 50

1863. April 10th.   A Bell, which cost $10.00, was put up in the rear of the Church.

1867, May 11th. It was proposed to rent the Vestry House at $50.00 a year for a boys and girls select school, but such a proposal would not be considered unless the school was a Parish School in aid of the church.

1867, 11th May. The Delegate to Convention was instructed to vote for a Division of the Diocese, so as to have a Bishop for the Eastern Shore of Maryland.

Sunday, 12.30 P. M., 18th October, 1868. L. M. Ricaud was elected Delegate and Josias Ringgold Alternate to go to Convention at Easton, Md., to assist at the Election of a Bishop for the Diocese of Easton, State of Maryland.

April 15th, 1869. Horatio Beck was elected Delegate and Josias Ringgold, Jr., alternate, to the Diocesan Convention, to meet in Easton, Md., on November 20th, 1868

Sunday, 27th June. Bishop Lay visited St. Paul's for the first time and confirmed six persons. On his tour he went to Still Pond, &c.

Sept. 14th, 1867. Morning and evening services to be held in the Church.

Aug. 31, 1870. Church debt over $1000.00.

Jan 14, 1875. No services to be held in St. Paul's on 5th Sunday in every month. Rector to employ them in Missionary Work in the Parish.

July 5th, 1875 The Vestry begged the Rector to have Services in the Church on 5th Sundays. Rector refused.

Feb. 1st, 1877. It seemed to be the unanimous opinion that the Rector shall be requested to give up the use of the 5th Sundays out of St. Paul's Church.

Easter Monday, 1875. Money received for previous year was $746.20.

July 5th, 1875. Vestry House to be fitted up for a Sunday School Room.

Sept. 7th, 1875. $100 voted for Roofing the Church.

CHURCH ON FIRE.

Easter Monday, 1875. A new policy of fire insurance on the Church was ordered, which had been neglected. The Vestry were forcibly reminded of this neglect, as coals had rolled out of the stove and fallen on the church floor, and part of the floor was entirely consumed by fire left over from Sunday Services. The Vestry record their gratitude to " Divine Providence that this venerated building was spared to us."

July 9th 1877. Vestry a good deal in debt on account of the Church. It was " hard times," &c. Some Voluntary Extraordinary effort of the members was proposed to meet the difficulty. Fairs were not to be thought of, or tolerated, only as a last resort. Some members offered to give $50.00 each, if some personal effort was made by others, sooner than have another Fair.

Easter Monday, 1878. Vestry voted that it meet once a month regularly. Any member not attending, or even 15 minutes late, to be fined $1 00. That Vestry meant business !

The same Vestry ordered that the Church Wardens should admonish persons who stand around the doors and windows after the beginning of the services. Such persons must be made to come into the church, or else the Wardens must make them go outside of the enclosure of the church-yard.

Dec. 5, 1879. Through means taken by Mrs. Hulme and Mrs. Ringgold, new stoves had been put in the Church, and the Church had been repaired and frescoed, at a cost of $300.00. Vestry in much difficulty as to money, and offered to pay one-half of the year's expenses, if the congregation would pay the other half

SUBSCRIPTIONS TO MEET THIS DIFFICULTY IN MARCH 28, 1880.

VESTRYMEN.

Josias Ringgold, Jr.,	$50 00	
Capt. W. J. Rasin	50 00	
T. A. Hulme	50 00	
Joseph Rasin	50 00	
George Beck	15 00	
James Rankin	25 00	
J. A. Schwearer	25 00	
Stevenson Constable	25 00	

WARDENS.

Geo. A. Jessop	20 00
T. W. Ringgold	5 00

MEMBERS.

Ben Taylor	5 00
Louis C. Ayres	5 00
Mrs. S. E. Page	15 00
Mrs. M. M. Beck	15 00
Jos. E. Gilpin	5 00
Mrs. A. M. Hurtt	25 00

Mrs. S. F. Jones	25 00
Mrs. Bogle	5 00
Mrs. Polly Willson	10 00
Mrs. A. C. Gamble	15 00
Miss Maria Gamble	5 00
Chas. G. Wheatley	15 00
Walter B. Strong	5 00
Henry Corson	10 00
Wm. Kline	5 00
Mrs. N. Voshell	5 00
Mr. N. Voshell	5 00
Marshall Jones	2 00
Chambers Jones	2 00
Harry Nichols	5 00
Wm. Francis	10 00
Harry Francis	5 00
Simpers Tarr	5 00
Wm. Ford	10 00
B. F. Beck	10 00

Total, $539.00, of which the Vestrymen subscribed $290.00. These subscribers comprise 8 Vestrymen and 27 Members.

Easter Monday, 29th March, 1880. The Rev'd Dr. Eccleston, of Staten Island, New York, offered to give a lecture at Tolchester for the benefit of the Church.

April 11, 1880. Thanks were tendered to Dr. Eccleston for his lectures on " Westminster Abbey," in London, England, on April 8th and 9th.

Thanks were tendered also to W. C. Eliason for the use of his hall, for the lectures, at Tolchester.

1877—Mrs. John Carvill Hynson presented to the church two chairs which had belonged to the Carvill Hynson family from early colonial times ; they are carved, straight-cane-backed paneled chairs, and have cane seats. They stand now just outside the Altar Railing.

13th July, 1882. Church floor to be repaired.

JULY 22d, 1882.—MEMORIAL OF GEORGE AND ROSA BECK'S CHILDREN.

A font cover of black walnut, carved, and surmounted by a Cross, was presented to St. Paul's Church by Mrs. Rosa Beck, on Easter day, 25th April, 1880, as a memorial of their deceased children, Rosa Harris Beck, born 15th April, 1880, died 1st July, 1881 ; and Clarence Benjamin Beck, born Oct., 1881, died 22d July, 1882. " Requiescat in Pace."

3d November, 1882. Cost of Church floor, and a porch to the Glebe house, $178.13.

30th May, 1883. Walk made in front of Church, and new Gates put to the entrance.

2d Nov., 1885. Organ moved in the Gallery, so as organist's back should not be to the Rector.

2d Nov., 1885. J. C. Wheatley appointed Delegate to Convention for the Election of a Bishop to succeed Bishop Lay, deceased.

Oct., 1888. Interior of Church neatly painted ; cost, $175.00.

16th Feb., 1890. Mrs. Sarah Jones, a former member, now in Baltimore, presented a handsome marble slab for the Communion Table. The Communion Table now in use (1893) is made out of this marble, with wood work out of the Old Holy Table built in with it.

16th Feb., 1890. Church newly carpeted throughout at $150.00.

22d Sept., 1890. Mrs. M. M. Beck presented Stove for Vestry house.

April, 1893. Shutters and Cornice of the Church painted ; new shingles put on the Chancel roof and the floor of Vestry Room repaired at a cost of $55.

SECTION IV.

CALL OF THE FIRST CLERGY.

July 24th, 1693. The Vestry requested Mr. Thomas Smith and Mr. Mich'l Miller to procure a minister for this Parish, and have in order thereto Desired them to go down to St. Mary's, where they are informed several are arrived with the Governor.

15th Sept., 1694. Mr. Lawrence Vanderbush having offered himself to officiate as Minister in this Parish, have agreed with the said Mr. Lawrence Vanderbush for one whole year, and to allow him the sum of Eight Thousand pounds of Tobacco.

Feb. 19th, 1695. Mr. Thos. Smith and Mr. Michael Miller were paid 450 pounds of Tobacco for the trip to St. Mary's.

Aug. 31, 1696. Mr. Vanderbush is spoken of as the late Minister of this parish. (by death).

July 2nd, 1697. This day came Mr. Stephen Bordley who produced an order from His Excellency, the Gov'r, to this Vestry, vizt :

Gent.—The Bearer hereof is Mr. Stephen Bordley, who is sent by the Right Hon'ble and Right Rev'd Father in God, Henry Lord Bishop of London, in order to officiate as a clergyman of the Church of England in this his Majestie's Province of Maryland ; I do therefore, in his Majestie's name appoint the said Mr. Stephen Bordley to officiate as a clergyman of the Church of England in the Parish of St. Paul's in Kent county. Given under my hand and Seal at the Port of Annapolis, the 23rd day of June, in the 9th year of the reign of our Sovereign Lord William the third, by the Grace of God, of England, Scotland, France and Ireland, King, defender of the Faith, &c., Anno Domini, 1697.   St. Paul's Parish, in Kent county,

These,   FR : NICHOLSON.   [SEAL.]

Which order being read Mr. Stephen Bordl.y is by this Vestry kindly received and accepted of, and likewise ordered by this Vestry that thanks be returned to His Excellency, the Gov'r, for his care and his kindness herein.

On July 2nd, 1697, Stephen Bordley by order of his Excellency Francis Nicholson was inducted into said Parish. Receiving the assessment of 40 lbs Tobacco per poll, according the underwritten acct.

Anno, 1687—By 337 Taxables, Sallery Deducted, 12806 lbs. Tobo.
```
        1698—By 491       "       "       "       18658    "
        1699—By 499       "       "       "       18962    "
        1700—By 548       "       "       "       20824    "
                                                  ------
                                                  71250    "
```

SECTION V.

LIST OF CLERGY AND LAY READERS OF ST. PAUL'S.

Rev'd Lawrence Vanderbush..................from 15th Sep., 1694, to Death.

Rev'd Stephen Bordley,..................from 23d June, 1697, to 25th Aug., 1700.

George Worsely, as Lay Reader as ⎫
the Law directs, till a minis- ⎪
ter doth come ; at 2500 lbs. To- ⎬ ...from 5th Sep., 1709, to 11th Apl., 1711.
bacco pr annum, ⎭

Rev'd Alex. Williamson,..................from 10th May, 1711, to 19th Nov., 1728.

No Records,..................from 1728 to 1754.

Rev'd James Sterling.................from 1754 to Death, on 10th Nov., 1763.

Thomas Slipper, Lay Reader, at 2500 lbs. Tobacco, by ⎫
his Excellencie's appointment and the recommen- ⎬ ...from 1764 to 1766.
dation of the Vestry, ⎭

Rev. Mr. —— Reade,..................from 1769 to

Rev. Colin Fergnson,..................from 1st Jan., 1797, to

Rev. George Dashiell, for every other Sunday, from 14th July, 1800, to

Rev. John Armstrong,..................from 1804 to July, 1805.

Rev. Simon Willmer..................from Feb., 1806, to June, 1808.

Lay Readers, Robert Dunn and William Willmer, from 26th June, 1808.

Rev'd Wm. H. Willmer, for every other ⎫
Sunday, ⎬ from Mar. 27, 1809, to Jan. 1, 1812.

Rev. Samuel H. Turner, every other Sunday, from 23d Feb., 1812, to Feb., 1815.

Rev. George Handy,..................from 7th Feb , 1815, to 23d Nov., 1816.

Rev. Mr. Cooper, ...from Mar., 1817, to

Rev. Mr. Walker, ...from Ap'l, 1818, to Ap'l, 1819.

Lay Reader. Mr. Lemuel Willmer, at $50 for the expenses of his horse, } .... from 1821, to

Rev. Timothy Clowes, L. L. D.................... ... from 1st May, 1824, to
No Record from the Rev'd Dr. Clowes' time till the time of the Rev'd Mr. Alberger, Rector for a short period in 1839.

Rev. F. W. Boyd, ($450 a year),........... ..from Nov., 1840, to 27th Dec. 1841.

Rev. Clement F. Jones. D. D.,... from 1841 to

Rev. Thomas B. Flower.. ....from 5th May, 1844, to 28th Mar., 1847.

Rev. Sam'l Robt. Gordon,......... ....from 30th Aug., 1847, to Sep., 1852.

Rev. Clement F. Jones. D. D.,......................from April, 1855, to Easter, 1857.

Rev. James Young......................from July 1st, 1858, to 28th Jan., 1860.

Rev. Andrew Sutton, Jr.,...................from 1st April, 1860, to 9th April, 1867.

Rev. E. A. H. Goodwin. Rector of } ....from May, 1867, to 26th Dec., 1867.
Chestertown,

Rev. Robert Wilson, M. D.,.................from 6th Sept., 1868, to 1st May, 1871.

Rev. E. G. Perryman, (with I. U.)....from 28th May, 1871, to 28th May, 1872.

Rev. C. J. Hendley, (with I. U.).............from 9th April, 1873, to March, 1874.

Rev. S. S. Hepburn, (with I. U.)......................................from 1874 to 1881.

Rev. Stephen C. Roberts, of Chester- } from 25th Sep., 1881, to May 22, 1882.
town, officiated pro. tem., every
other Sunday,

Rev. Henry Wall, D. D.,.........................from 22d May, 1882, to Sept., 1887.

Rev. William Munford, (with I. U.).....from 29th April, 1888, to 7th Oct., 1889.

Rev. S. C. Roberts, Rector of Chester- } from 2d Feb., 1890, to 13th Ap'l, 1890.
town, every other Sunday,

Rev. Geo. C. Sutton, (with I. U)......from 13th April, 1890, to 10th Mar., 1892.

Rev. Chris. T. Denroche, (with I. U.)......from 1st May, 1892, is here in 1893.

Mr. Linington Roberts Shewell was made Lay Reader on 10th March, 1892. He read the Service and preached a Sermon every Sunday in St. Paul's Church from 10th March, 1892, to 1st May, 1892, while the parish was without a Rector. Since then he has admirably assisted the Rector (Chris. T. Denroche) by reading the Service every Sunday at St. Paul's and at Rock Hall Mission, when Service was held there.

SECTION VI.

PEWS RENTED AND PEWS FREE AND ENVELOPE SYSTEM.

1698. 500 lbs. Tobacco for 4 seats in a pew.

1714. 1000 lbs. Tobacco for each pew, said pew to be the property of the buyer and his heirs forever.

1841. 16 Front Pews, each $15 00.
"   16 next to front, each $10 00.
"   The Remainder, $5 00.

Choice for Pews in 1841 was by lot. The Pews were drawn by lot on July 23d, 1842, after the Restoration of the Church in 1841. Tickets were numbered in accordance with the number of the subscribers. The subscriber who drew No. 1 had the first choice, and No. 2 the second, and so on. The plan of these Pews is pasted in the end of the oldest book of the Records of Vestry from 1693 to 1726, marked No. 2.

1862.   Pew Rental nearly $500 00.

April 1, 1864, to April 1, 1865.   Pew Rental for the year $545 00.

April 1, 1865, to April 1, 1866.   "   "   "   "   " $97 00.

April 1, 1866, to April 1, 1867.   '   "   "   "   "   445 00.

From 1862, Pews were sold to the highest bidder.

In January, 1866, it was recorded that out of the 45 Pews only 15 are actually rented.

Pews were made Free on 1st May, 1870.

Pews Rented again on 8th July, 1872.   14 of the front pews in middle block at $30.00 each ; the rest, being rear pews in middle block, at $25 00 each ; 14 of the front pews in side blocks at $10.00 each ; the rest, being rear pews in side blocks, at $5.00 each.

9th Aug., 1872.   The average Rental of the whole of the Pews was between $500.00 and $600 00.

Envelope System of Collections adopted, 1876, March 10th, under 4 conditions :

1st. Average of amount of Communion Alms deducted.

2d. Rector's Salary to be deducted.

3d. Current Church Expenses deducted.

4th. Surplus to go to Missions and Church Repairs.

1876, March 24th. $626.90 subscribed as per Envelope System.

1877, Feb. 1st.   Great deficiency up to this time under the Envelope System.

1877, April 2d.   Envelope System only "not an *utter* failure," as the sum of $410.64 was collected by it since 24th March, 1876.

1882, 10th April.   Proposal to Rent pews was not carried : the church was supported by Voluntary Subscriptions.

1885, 6th December.   Envelope System again adopted, but it worked very unsatisfactorily. The Books were not kept properly, as no one account was kept distinct, and payments were not made by many ; consequently, on 1st April, 1887, the Envelope System was abolished, and the Church was then, as it has been since up to this date, supported by Voluntary Contributions and Subscriptions.

SECTION XII.

THE CEMETERY.

"ETERNAL REST GRANT UNTO THEM, O LORD, AND LIGHT PERPETUAL SHINE
UPON THEM."

The oldest stone-marked grave in St. Paul's Cemetery has inscribed on its *foot-stone :*

> Here lies ye body of Daniel Coley.
>
> He departed this life Oct. ye 20, 1729.
>
> Cut by John Godfrey.

The *head-stone* is as follows :

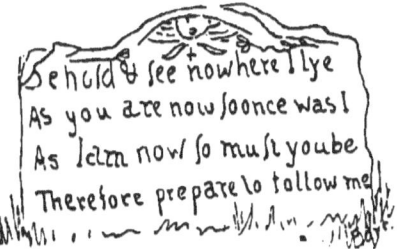

Behold & see nowhere I lye
As you are now Joonce was I
As Iam now Jo muJt yoube
Therefore prepare to follow me

The next oldest has : "Here lyes ye Body of Even Evans. He departed this life June ye 30, 1735."

The next is of Benjamin Vickers, Esq., 1790.

There are a number of very old graves, with rough head and foot-stones, but which bear no inscription at all.

*   *   *   *   *   *   *   *   *   *

At 9 A. M., June 1, 1863, Mr. Eben F. Perkins proceeded, under direction of the Vestry, to lay out Walks and Burial Lots in the Cemetery. At 8 A. M. Tuesday the work was continued until 4.30 P. M.

On 28th March, 1864, the Rev. Andrew Sutton and L. M. Ricaud were given exclusive control of the Cemetery.

In 1865. L. M. Ricaud had sole control.

Dr. L. M. Ricaud and Geo. D. S. Handy were the instigators and first workers in beautifying the Cemetery at this time.

The work then fell for some time to Dr. Ricaud.

Up to December, 1868. Dr. Ricaud, in leveling, stumping, cleaning, fencing, &c., in the Cemetery, laid out $549.00. He had $162.00 worth of trees planted. In 1876 he made a draft of the Cemetery plot.

In 1878, on 22d April. Under a new survey by Mr. John V. Crosby, at the direction of G. D. S. Handy and Chas. G. Ricaud, a new draft of the Cemetery plot was made at a cost of $20.00.

April 22, 1878. By Bequest of the late Mrs. Augusta Browne, the sum of $50.00 was left in her will to be perpetually invested for the purpose of keeping her grave in proper order.

Too much gratitude for Cemetery improvement cannot be held towards Dr. L. M. Ricaud and George D. S. Handy.

In an obituary Resolution of Vestry, in 1874, there occurs the following words in connection with Mr. George D. S. Handy and the Cemetery of St. Paul's Church : " Resolved, that always working to beautify the Cemetery grounds, where her Beloved sleep, *that* Cemetery, so endeared to us all, shall be, and is, his most fitting Monument."

April 22d, 1880. The Treasurer in charge of the Cemetery was directed to notify lot-holders who have not paid for their lots that unless their lots are paid for, no more graves will be allowed to be dug within them ; also to notify Sexton not to dig any more graves in such lots.

STEVENSON CONSTABLE, Register.

1880, March 9th. No more lots to be sold in the Cemetery except for cash.

April 10, 1882, and April 28, 1882. There were 48 unsold lots ; a graded price was put upon each one according to location.

April 7, 1890. T. R. Strong to have sole care of Mrs. Augusta Browne's lot and to spend $3.00 each year on it

Aug. 27, 1870. A man to to be hired as Sexton and to work in the Cemetery at a Salary, and Lot holders to be charged each $1.00 a year for the care of their lots. Bills for collection were divided among the Vestrymen, and each Vestryman was to be responsible for non-collections, or to show good cause.

Sept. 16, 1891. Thomas Hill, of Baltimore, wrote that a lady desired to furnish $300.00, the interest of which was to pay for the care of her lot, and any balance to be applied on the Cemetery fence.

April 18, 1892. Receipts, $283.25 ; expenses, $196.48 ; due for lots, $95.00 ; due for grave digging, $16.00 ; due for care of lots in 1891, $24.00.

April 3d, 1893. Receipts, $246.50 ; expenses, $220.95.

CEMETERY FENCE, AS NOW ROUND CEMETERY.

1884, 29th July. Messrs Hulme and George Bell were made a committee to report the cost of an iron fence, and to solicit subscriptions for it. (See Appendix).

1888, 13th May. Mr. George Beck submitted a plan, the cost of which in carrying out was to be $1500.00, complete.

1889, 7th August. A plank fence refused, and Mr. George Beck to supply a sample of his proposed fence.

1890, 29th January. A cheap fence at $400.00 proposed.

1890, 22d September. A wire netting fence had been put up at a cost of $630.44. This is substantial and of excellent appearance. An iron piping rail is put up a few feet in front of the fence for tying horses to.

The building and the collecting funds for this fence is due to the loving exertions of Mr. George Beck.

1893. The cemetery is now in most excellent condition, thoroughly clean and well cared for. It is under the management of Mr. Thomas W. Skirven. Between nature's grand provision and art's careful supply, this Cemetery of St. Paul's is second to none for quiet grandeur and exquisite beauty. It is situated on the summit of a gentle slope, with a pretty, bright stream of water at the foot of the hill, while the dear old Church, at its brow, rises from its 200 years of foundation in a call of peace and rest with God. Great giant oaks make the scene majestically beautiful from the hand of nature, and art has done her part in promoting most sweet loveliness. The tree tops of the great giant oak trees tower their lofty heads as reaching for the skies, and stretch out their tops as fingers ever pointing heavenwards. Their great lower limbs reach out their wondrous length in unusual size and strength, as though typical of the Great loving arm of the Good God, stretched out over His own Sacred Acre, in merciful care of His faithful departed holy dead. Hosts of evergreen and other trees and shrubs are in irregular beauty all around the grounds. The graves are all neat and well cared for, the walks clean and hard. Flowers in abundance adorn the scene and bright green grass everywhere colors and closely covers the whole Cemetery. May it long remain a home of beauty for the bodies of our much loved departed members and all true friends.

SECTION XIII.

THE GLEBE.

Oct. 21, 1859. On motion, it was resolved that the Vestry purchase the farm called Mount Pleasant, (commonly known as the Tilden farm), for a Glebe, from R. Hynson, Esq., Trustee. Agreed that it be bought by James P. Wickes, Geo. D. S. Handy, Horatio Beck and T. W. Ringgold, in trust for the Parish, at a cost of Twelve hundred dollars, payable in 6, 12, 18 and 24 months from 1st Jan'y, 1860. A subscription for payment of it was then taken in writing. H. W. Carvill, James P. Wickes, Horatio Beck, Thos. W. Ringgold and Geo. D. S. Handy subscribed $100.00 each, and paid it; Judge E. F. Chambers paid $50.00; Dr. B. F. Houston, $50.00; Wm. P. Francis, $25.00; George B. Westcott, $50.00, paid; Richard Hynson, $25.00, paid; L. M. Ricaud, 70.00, paid $35.00; William T. Skirven, $25.00, paid in bricks; James Brown, $50.00, $25.00 paid.

An account entry records that the Glebe was settled for in 1865.

April 11, 1863. Ordered that the Division line between the Glebe and Isaiah C. Taylor be surveyed, to ascertain the quantity of land he purchased. Then to have the line fixed between N. Voshell and the Glebe, the Vestry to determine as to selling him a number of acres, or as to moving the line, and give and take, so as to straighten the line.

April 22, 1867. Resolved to build on the west end of the house, already built, a suitable building for the Parish Rector. House to be 20x28 feet; 10 foot hall, 2 stories high; lower story 10 feet ceiling, upper story 9 feet; 4 dormer windows, 2 in front and 2 at back; Shutters throughout the main building.

Mr. Beck reported, on behalf of the Ladies of the Parish, $500.00 cash, and $500.00 more to be received towards, and for, the Glebe Rectory. The old building to be repaired and raised 2 feet higher from the ground; cellar to be 6 ft. 6 in. high and 26x28 feet in length and breadth.

11th Dec., 1868. The Rectory and Repairs cost $2767.40 cents. The value of the whole house was estimated at $3567.40.

Aug. 26, 1869. A committee of Vestry was ordered to negotiate the sale of 40 acres of the Glebe Land, and to apply the proceeds to the extinction of the debt of the parish and to the improvement of the remaining property.

29th Dec., 1869. Mr. Clark Taylor offered $20.00 an acre for 40 more acres of the Glebe Land, which was thought too small a figure.

5th May, 1870. Rector, the Rev'd R. Wilson, M. D., said that the Glebe could not be sold unless the Rector's consent was given.

17th Nov., 1871. Committee of Vestry had contracted with I. C. Taylor to sell him a part of the Glebe at $20.00 an acre. Glebe lot to be surveyed.

19th Feb., 1872. The Rev. Mr. Perryman might cultivate for his own use the Glebe land not otherwise disposed of.

22d May, 1872. Messrs. Taylor and Skirven, with the Vestry, were to sign and fix the Deed for Glebe land sold them. Mr. Taylor objected to Surveyor Crosby's lines, but agreed to settle the whole matter next Monday.

On 9th Sept., 1871. Vestry determined to sell 40 or 50 acres of Glebe land at a minimum price of $20 an acre. Line to run parallel with west boundary of Glebe lands. Also to see what the land in front of the Glebe can be bought for. Soon after, in 1872, (See Record Book 6, page 105), 36 acres, 1 rood and 33 perches were sold at $20.00 an acre; total, $729.12. Sold to I. C. Taylor.

24th April, 1875. Resolved, to rent the Glebe so as to draw revenue.

Two acres, more or less, were sold to Mr. T. W. Skirven for $30.00, part to be paid in cedar posts and chestnut rails, delivered at the line of a Glebe fence, and the Balance in cash.

17th Feb., 1876. Glebe to be rented. Capt. W. J. Rasin, T. A. Hulme and James Rankin to be a committee in charge.

2d March, 1876. Charles J. Wheatley agrees to Rent or Lease the Glebe for 1876, 1877 and 1878.

11th Dec., 1878. The Rev'd S. S. Hepburn to treat with the Minister and Trustees of the M. E. (colored) Church on buying a piece of land in front of the Rectory Gate, and on which their church formerly stood.

31st Dec., 1879.   The Rector requested to be allowed control of the Glebe Lands himself.

9th Oct., 1881.   Glebe rented to Mr. Wheatley for one-half the grain

16th March, 1882.   A contract for Glebe Lands with Mr. Hague was considered and referred back for alterations.

29th Oct., 1881.   The Glebe land was rented to Mr. Simpers Tarr.

28th April.   A proposal to sell the Glebe Lands and buy land out of Dr. Houston's farm, failed.

3d Nov., 1882.   Fencing repairs done at $68.42.

7th Feb., 1883.   Glebe Rented to Mr. Hagee.

2d Nov., 1885.   Only 557 out of 813 peach trees growing.

20th Dec., 1886.   Tenant Reported Glebe Lands too poor to grow peaches.

14th March, 1887.   Mr. George Bell offered to supply Peach trees and wait for pay till they bore fruit.

11th April, 1887.   Mr. George Bell supplied 1000 Peach trees.

22d Jan., 1888.   Glebe Rented to Mr. LeCount at $125.00.

10th Dec., 1888.   Glebe Rented to Mr. John Joiner at $125.00.

13th Mar., 1889.   2,500 Shingles to be put on Glebe House.

1893.   Glebe now rented to Mr. James E. Jewell.

ADDENDA.

The last Burial in St. Paul's Cemetery was that of Helen Denroche, the wife of the present Rector. She had been attending a meeting of arrangements for the 1893 Bi-centennial celebration of the Parish, and died suddenly in the carriage on her way home.

MEMORIALS.

The Chandelier in the Nave of St. Paul's Church, Kent county, Md., was given in the year 1882 by Miss Maria L. Gamble, in memory of her two sisters, Anna Catharine, wife of Josias Ringgold, Jr., and Mary Elizabeth, wife of Edgar H. Strong.

The Chandelier in the Chancel of the Church was given by Mrs. Ann C. Gamble, in memory of her sisters, Mary M. Beck and Sarah E. S. Page, on 17th May, 1893.

The two Standard Lamps in the Chancel were presented by Mrs. Sarah Jones at the same time as the Altar Slab, on the 16th February, 1890.

SECTION IX.

OBITUARY NOTICES.

JAMES FRIZBY FREEMAN.

June 10th, 1846.

Resolved. That the humble and consistent walk, and the zealous and unpretending labors of our lamented Brother, (a member of this Vestry), entitle him to a place in the recollections of this parish.

Resolved, That we deeply sympathize with the bereaved family.

Resolved, That we wear crape upon our left arm for the space of three months as a tribute of respect to his memory.

By order of the Vestry.   THOMAS B. FLOWER, Rector.

THOMAS MILLER.

April 9th, 1849.

An esteemed Brother and Friend, and for very many years a member of our Vestry.

JACOB THEODORE FREEMAN.

April 21st, 1851.

The Vestry notice with deep regret the death of their highly esteemed friend, Jacob Theodore Freeman, whose health had been so impaired as to compel him to retire from the Vestry last year.

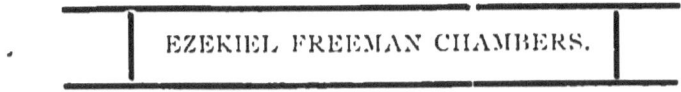

EZEKIEL FREEMAN CHAMBERS.

Feb. 5th, 1867.

He was born in Chestertown, Kent county, Md., on the 28th February, 1788, and died in Chestertown on 30th January, 1866, in the Seventy-ninth year of his age. "Requiescat in Pace." God Bless You.

He was a kind and charitable Christian, a good and useful citizen: was more than 40 years president of the Board of Visitors and Governor of Washington College, Chestertown: many years a most devoted Churchman, whose sympathy was ever most acutely sensitive to the interests of The Holy Catholic Church and to the cause of Christianity generally. His loss will be irreparable to the Church and to the Community in which he lived. May he rest in peace and sleep with God.

Lawrence M. Ricaud, Register.

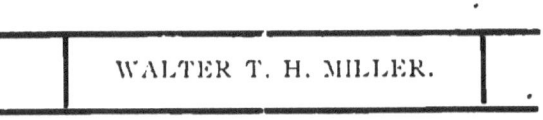

WALTER T. H. MILLER.

October 12, 1868.

The Register is directed to communicate with the family of the late Walter T. H. Miller, late Vestryman of this Parish, the assurance of our sincere sympathy and condolence in their bereavement of one who has been so long associated with us in promoting the interests and welfare of the Church.

Resolved, that we wear black crape upon the left arm for 30 days, as a mark of respect for the late Walter T. H. Miller.

Lawrence M. Ricaud, Register.

JAMES PAGE WICKES.

January 11, 1869.

Resolved, that the Wardens and Vestrymen wear crape upon the left arm for 30 days as a slight testimonial of sincere respect for our late friend and brother Vestryman, James Page Wickes, the sincere friend and polished gentleman, of whom it had been most truly said: "*He was one of Nature's Noblemen.*"

Resolved, that a copy of this resolution be forwarded to the family of the deceased, with the assurance of sincere sympathy and condolence in their sad bereavement.

Lawrence M. Ricaud, Register.

LAWRENCE M. RICAUD, M. D.

August 19th, 1879.

WHEREAS, it has pleased Almighty God, in His inestimable Wisdom, to remove from his earthly usefulness our late esteemed Friend and brother Vestryman, Dr. Lawrence M. Ricaud,—

Resolved, That we shall long miss from our meetings Dr. Ricaud's kindly presence and his active zeal in promoting all the interests of this Parish ; and that while in other relations of life we must deeply lament the decease of one endeared to us by so many high personal qualities, most especially as Vestryman of St. Paul's do we deplore the loss to the Church of those valuable services which were so willingly at her command.

Resolved, That we offer our heartfelt sympathy to his bereaved and sorrowing family, and that we wear the usual badge of mourning for thirty days.

Resolved, That these Resolutions be published in the County Papers, and a copy of them be sent to the family, and that a blank page in the minutes be inscribed to the memory of the deceased.

In Memoriam :

DR. LAWRENCE MILLER RICAUD,

Late Vestryman and Register

of St. Paul's Parish.

Obt. Aug. 18th, 1869.

DR. RICAUD'S MONUMENT.

May 5th, 1870. Moved by Mr. Horatio Beck and adopted, that Mr. George D. S. Handy be a committee to take charge of the money subscribed in this parish to erect a suitable monument over the remains of the late Dr. L. M. Ricaud, and have it properly placed as soon as possible.

GEORGE D. S. HANDY, Register.

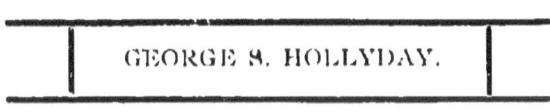

GEORGE S. HOLLYDAY.

20th March, 1870.

Resolved, That the Vestry wear the usual badge of mourning 30 days in respect to the memory of the late George S. Hollyday, and that this practice be adopted as a Standing Resolution on all occasions of a like character.

R. WILSON, Sect'y.

T. W. RINGGOLD, Esq.

In Memoriam : T. W. Ringgold, Esq.

WHEREAS, it has pleased an all-wise Providence to remove from this life our esteemed Friend and brother Vestryman, T. W. Ringgold, Esq.,—

Resolved, The Church and community have sustained a great loss, and we deeply deplore his death.

Resolved, We offer our sympathy and condolence to his bereaved family and wear the usual badge of mourning for thirty days.

GEORGE D. S. HANDY, Reg.

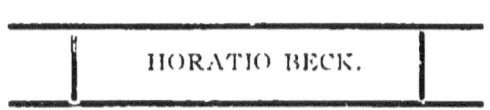

HORATIO BECK.

Departed this life on the 12th day of June, 1874.

Who was for many years of his life actively engaged in forwarding the interests and promoting the welfare of St. Paul's Church.

Mr. Beck has been connected with this Church as a Vestryman since early manhood, and has acted as Treasurer for a long time and with entire satisfaction to his associates, freely devoting his time and means to further the Church's prosperity. His decease leaves a great blank in our midst, that will be felt for a long time.

Therefore, whereas, it has pleased Almighty God to take from us Mr. Horatio Beck, a Vestryman of this Church,—

Resolved, That while we bow in submission to the will of God, we cannot refrain from expressing our grief at the double loss we have sustained as Vestrymen and individuals.

Resolved, That in Mr. Beck the Vestry has lost its most useful and honored member, while we as individuals have been called to surrender a friend endeared to us alike by memories of the past and by his noble qualities.

Resolved, That this parish to which he belonged, and the community in which he lived, has lost a man whose place cannot be easily filled : a man whose soundness of judgment and devotion to the welfare of the Church has won for his opinions the respect of all.

Resolved, That we tender to his family our heartfelt sympathy in their afflicting bereavement, and that we wear the usual badge of mourning for thirty days.

Resolved, That a copy of these resolutions be sent to his family and entered upon the Journal in memorial of the deceased.

CHARLES G. RICAUD, Registrar.

1874. In Memoriam.

GEORGE D. S. HANDY.

WHEREAS, it hath pleased our Heavenly Father to take from us our greatly esteemed Friend and faithful Register of this Parish, George D. S. Handy, Esq,—

Resolved, That it becomes us as a Christian to bow in humble submission to His decree and say "Thy Will be done."

Resolved, That in the Vestry we shall always miss him for his extreme courtesy and firmness of manner in our deliberations, as well as for his practical and conservative views in all things pertaining to the welfare of this Church and Parish.

Resolved, That always working to promote the interests of this Church and to beautify the Cemetery grounds where her beloved sleep, *that* Cemetery, so endeared to us all, shall be, and is, his most fitting monument.

Resolved, That a copy of these Resolutions be sent to his family as a memento of our abiding sympathy with them in their time of affliction.

T. A. HULME.
C. G. RICAUD.

December 14th, 1876.

CAPTAIN JOHN CARVILL HYNSON.

WHEREAS, our Heavenly Father has taken from among us our esteemed associate, Captain John Carvill Hynson, the oldest Vestryman of this Church and the Representative of a family that has been intimately connected with the working of this Church and Vestry in Early Colonial times,—

Resolved, That while in his loss we recognize the hand of The Father "Who doeth all things well," we yet miss the presence of our friend and of one who was always ever ready to aid in all good works, and who by his conscientious discharge of duty gave evidence that he had indeed the intersts of the Church at heart.

Resolved, That we tender to his bereaved family our sincere sympathies in their affliction, remembering that while *they lose* an affectionate husband and relation, the *Church loses* an earnest supporter, while the *Vestry loses* a quiet worker and true friend.

Resolved, That as a token of our respect, the Wardens and Vestry shall wear the usual badge of mourning upon the left arm for the space of thirty days.

Resolved, That a copy of these Resolutions be sent to the afflicted family and entered upon the Records of St. Paul's Church.

Committee : { Chas. G. Ricaud,
{ George T. Hollyday.

April 3rd, 1893.

STEVENSON CONSTABLE.

WHEREAS, it has pleased our Heavenly Father, in His inscrutable Wisdom, to remove from our midst our dear friend and brother in Christ, Stevenson Constable, be it

Resolved, That the Vestry and congregation of St. Paul's Parish desire to testify their sincere sorrow at the death of Mr. Constable, and to bear witness' to those Christian graces and sterling qualities of mind and heart which have endeared him to them all By his death a void is left that can never be adequately filled He will be sadly missed in our advisory councils, having been a member of St. Paul's Vestry for 15 years, and Registrar for 14 years. He was ever ready and foremost in all good works—a loyal son of the Church, loving her laws and upholding her dignity wise and temperate in counsel, his influence for good was widely felt, and it is with a deep sense of our great loss, that we place this tribute of respect and affection on the grave of that true Christian gentleman.

Resolved, That we extend our heartfelt sympathies to the bereaved widow and children of the deceased, trusting that the Divine Love which has so chastened them in depriving them of the loving husband and tender and affectionate father, will, in Its own good time, enable them to bow in humble submission and resignation to God's will, and fill their sad hearts with that peace which passeth all understanding.

Resolved, That these resolutions be entered upon the minutes of the meeting and that a copy of them be forwarded to the family of the deceased, and also be inserted in the *Kent News* and *Transcript.*

BY ORDER OF THE VESTRY.

These Resolutions were adopted by a rising vote.

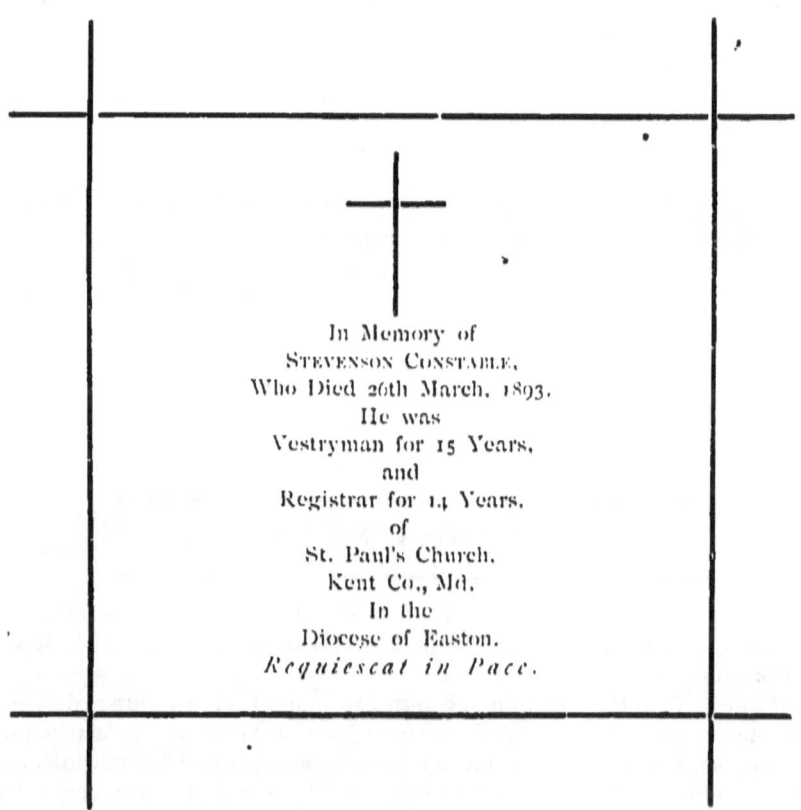

In Memory of
STEVENSON CONSTABLE,
Who Died 26th March, 1893.
He was
Vestryman for 15 Years,
and
Registrar for 14 Years,
of
St. Paul's Church,
Kent Co., Md.
In the
Diocese of Easton.
Requiescat in Pace.

APPENDIX.

RECORD BOOKS, THE PROPERTY OF ST. PAUL'S CHURCH IN MAY, 1893.

No. 1. From 1679 to 1800. Being an old Fragmentary Book (with broken binding) of Births, Baptisms, Marriages and Burials, arranged in alphabetical order; with some various entries at end of book.

No. 2. From 30th Jany., 1693, to 11th April, 1726. Being a rebound old Book of Vestry Meeting Records, inscribed on fly leaf "Transcriptions of Former Vestry Proceedings."

A plan of the disposition of pews, as allotted to the subscribers in 1842, is inserted at end of this book.

No. 3. From 1725 to 1738. Being "The Book of Accounts belonging to the Vestry of St. Paul's Parish, in Kent county, Anno 1727."

Vestry Meetings from May ye 13th to Nov. ye 19th, 1728, and one of Feb. 18th, 1799, are at close of book.

No. 4. From 11th April, 1811, to 3th May, 1860. Being a record of Baptisms, Confirmations, Marriages and Burials.

No. 5. From 25th July, 1800, to 8th January, 1862. Being Record of Proceedings of Vestry. Some accounts, and some lists of Church Officers are at the beginning and end of this book, and also at about 20 pages from the end of it. Some loose papers are secured on inside of last cover.

No. 6. From 28th April, 1862, to 1st April, 1882. Being Records of Vestry Meetings; also a few entries of Baptisms, Marriages and Burials, and lists of Church officers.

No. 7. From Sep., 1868, to Oct., 1889. Being Records of Families, Baptisms, Confirmations, Communicant, Marriages and Burials.

No. 8. From 15th April, and now in use. Being ditto of items in No. 7.

No. 9. From 10th April, 1882; and now in use. Record of Vestry Meetings.

ST PAUL'S, CONNECTED WITH SHREWSBURY PARISH, AND SASSAFRAS CHURCH, IN 1696 AND 1707, Etc.

In 1696 the Vestry inquired about a letter they had written to Shrewsbury Parish, in "Cecil" county, demanding of them the tobacco due by them to the Estate of Mr. Lawrence Vanderbush. From this it appears that at that time Shrewsbury Parish was in Cecil county, and that the Rev. Mr. Vanderbush ministered there as well as in St. Paul's Parish.

Entry of Dec. 12, 1698: Whereas, as this Vestry is in prospect of getting 7,500 pounds of tobacco from Cecil county, thinks it not necessary to assess a parish tax this year.

11th Feb., 1699. Notes were drawn on Sheriff Mr. John Carvill, of Cecil county, for the revenue due to Mr. Stephen Bordley, fourty pounds pr poll. Mr. Bordley was the second minister at St. Paul's, Feb. 24, 1702. A petition was presented to the Vestry of St. Paul's from the gentlemen of the Parish of Shrewsbury, in Cecil county, requesting Mr. Stephen Bordley to preach there every third Sunday.

Jan. 9th, 1706-7. It was moved by Mr. Stephen Bordley to continue preaching the first Sabbath in the month at Sassafras Church. The Vestry deferred their consideration till their next meeting.

Sep. 6, 1701. Mr. Harris doth move to the Justices of Cecil county to assess a Parish tax for that part of the parish lying in Cecil county, for the repairing and to enlarge the church, at 10 lbs. tobacco pr poll, according to Act of Assembly.

I. U. In 1883, and for some few years before then, and at other intervals, St. Paul's has been connected with Christ Church, I. U. The proper name of the Church in I. U. district is Christ Church. But there happened to be a boundary stone on a corner in that locality, marked I. U., which were the initials of the name of the owner of the land. In this way the place became called I. U., and the Church became called I. U. likewise

MINISTER'S PLANTATION.

On April 10th, 1710. There is an entry in the Record as follows: Ordered that the Clerk sett up a Note at East Mill to give Notice that the Plantation which belongs to the Minister is to be Lett.

MEMO. OF A SALE OF A PEW.

Kent ss.: I, Edw'd Plestoe, of the County af'sd, do her by sell, assign and make over to Thomas Smith, of s'd county, his heirs and assigns for ever, all my part in the Pew in the Parish Church of St. Paul's, in the co'ty af'sd, Having rec'd Full Satisfaction for the same. Witness my hand and seal this third day of Jan'ry, 1711.

EDWARD PLESTOE. SEAL.|

Witness: J. (X) YARDLEY and J. (X) WOODALL.

PEWS AND PEW-HOLDERS AND SEAT-HOLDERS IN 1720.

No. 1. Mr. Alex. Williamson,
Col. Nathaniel Hynson,

No. 2. Col. Thos. Smyth,

No. 3. John March,
Solomon Wright,

No. 4. James Smyth,
Thos. Bown,

No. 5. Jas. Harris, Esq.

No. 6. Col. Edw'd Scott,

No. 7. Major Wm. Pott,
Rich'd Simmonds,

No. 8. John Moll,
Wm. Bateman,

No. 9. Sam'l Thomas,
Edw'd Davis,
John Evans,

No. 10. Simon Willmer,
Thomas Piner,

No. 11. John Fulston,
Rich'd Fulston,
Wm. Jones,
John Williams,

No. 12. Wm. Worrell,
Sam'l Tovey,

No. 13. Rebecca Willmer,
Thos. Ringgold,
Chas. Hynson,

No. 14. Wm. Frisby,
James Frisby,

No. 15. Wm. Glanville,
Wm. Pope,

No. 16. Thomas Crawford,
Anne Frisby,

No. 17. Oliver Higgenbottom,
John Green,
John Rolph,

No. 18. Marmaduke Tilden,
Thos. Hynson,

No. 19. Arthur Miller,
Edw'd Worrell,

No. 20. George Moore,
John Fanning,

No. 21. St. Legia Codd,
Hans Hanson,

No. 22. Daniel Duffy,
John Hynson,

No. 23. James Murphey,
Jacob Glann,

No. 24. Michael Hacket,
Philip Davis,

No. 25. Ebenezer Blackston,
John Blackston,

No. 26. John Rogers,
John Tilden,

No. 27. Micha'd Miller,
Sam'd Berry

No. 28. Robt. Dunn,
Wm. Dunn,

No. 29. John Taylor,
Wm. Simcocks,

No. 30. W ... ... ,
Chas. Ringgold,

No. 31. Edw'd Rogers, Jur.,
Sam'l Wickes,

No. 32. George Hanson,
Fred'k Hanson,

No. 33. For the Minister,
Thos. Bordley,
Stephen Bordley,

No. 34. Rich'd Fillingham,
Sam'l Goodin,
Ed. Jarvis

TOBACCO — £. S. D.—AND DOLLARS.

The mode of keeping accounts begins to be changed in January, 1798, from Tobacco to Pounds-Shillings and Pence, (£. S. D.,) The first mention of Dollars is on the 27th of October, 1800.

In 1762, a book for vestry use cost 800 pounds tobacco and seven shillings and six pence (written 7s. 6d.)

— ---

COST OF BUILDING VESTRY HOUSE.

Vestry House, built in 1766. The allowance for building the Vestry House (in front of the Church), 20,000 pounds of Tobacco. It was commenced in 1766 and completed in 1767. The account for cost of the Vestry House was rendered by Joseph Nicholson, Esq., Sheriff.

On May 12th, 1797, is the following account:

RICHARD HURTT TO THE VESTRY.

		£ S D
Dr. May, 1797. To cash		£28.0s.5½d.
		£ S D
Cr. May 12, 1797. By 8,000 Cypress Shingles, at £1.10s.11d		12 7 4
By 2,000 ft. inch plank, at 9s. 6d. per hundred		9 10 0
By 200 ft. of inch and ½ plank at 15s		1 10 0
By expenses in Baultimore		18 1½
By cash returned		3 15
		£28 0 5½

But what this material was used for is not recorded ; most likely it was for the Vestry House.

SAMPLE OF ACCOUNT IN TOBACCO IN 1734.

Mr. John Gresham.	Dr.		Per Contra.		Cr.
1734. Sheriff.	lbs. Tobacco		1733.		lbs. Tobacco.
To brought from fo. 24	4120		By order payable to Thomas Bordley		1150
To assessment of Ten pounds per poll on			By do, payable to Mr. Joseph Young		200
1176 Taxables	11760		1735.		
To 9 Taxables omitted, at 10 lbs. per poll	90		By years sallery, at 5 pr. ct. on 5845		
	15970		Tobacco		292½
			By Vestries order to Thomas Bordley		1000
			By do to Mary Mackey		800
			By do to Thos. Bordley in 1734		1000
			By do to Mary Mackey		800
			By do to Simon Wilmer		1000
			By commission for collecting 11760 at		
			5 pr. ct.		588
			By 4 Taxables returned in the consta-		
			ble's list		140
			By the Vestries order, payable to		
			Geo. Clark		500
			1737		
			By Tobacco paid Wm. Copper, by or-		
			der of the Vestry		180
					15950
			By Balance		20
	15910				15970½
Pounds of Tobacco.			Pounds of Tobacco.		

SALARIES OF CHURCH OFFICERS.

CLERGY. In 1694, $8,000; in 1697, 12,806; in 1698, 18,658; in 1699, 18,962; a 1700, 20,821 pounds of Tobacco. In 1840, $450; in 1844, $300; in 1858, $500; in 1862, $500 and hor e and carriage; in 1864, $600; in 1865, $700; in 1871, $600 and house and garden, pastur for hor e and cow, hors e, carriag e and fire-wood ; in 1873, $600 and do.; in 1878, $500 and do.; in 1882, $61 , Rectory, garden and pasture; from 1888 to 1893, $400, house, horse and f d, and carriage.

LAY READER, in 1711, 600 lbs. Tobacco per annum; in 1764, 2500 do.; in 1765, 1000 do.; in 1766, 2500 do.

REGISTER, in 1756, 750 lbs. Tobacco per annum ; in 1772, 1000 do.

VESTRY CLERK, in 1721, 600 lbs. Tobacco per annum.

ORGANIST, Prof. George Minnick, 1863, $25.00; do., 1864, $50.00; d r. T. Eagle, 1896, $100.00; Miss Laura Harris, 1866, $100.00.

SEXTON, in 1720, 600 lbs. Tobacco per annum ; in 1721, 500 do.; in 1750, 850 do.; in 1765, 1000 do.; in 1773, £15, or say $75 per annum.

FORM OF OATH FOR CHURCH OFFICERS AFTER THE REVOLU-TION, IN 1776.

June 5th, 1779. This day qualified by taking the oath of Fidelity and oath of office, Morgan Hurtt, Register; Mr. Richard Lloyd, Mr. James Dunn, Mr. John Sutton, Mr. Robert Cruikshank, Vestrymen.   (Signed) "MORGAN HURTT CHURCH."

I (A. B.) do swear that I do not hold myself bound to yield any allegiance or obedience to the King of Great Britain, his heirs or successors, and that I will be true and faithful to the State of Maryland, and will to the utmost of my power support, maintain and defend the freedom and the Independence thereof, and the Government as now established, against all open enemies and secret and traiterous conspiracies; and will use my utmost endeavours to disclose and make known to the Governor, or some one of the Judges or Justices thereof, all treasons or trait rous conspiracies, attempts or combinations against this State or the Government thereof which may come to my knowledge. So help me God.   MORGAN HURTT, Register.

RICHARD LLOYD,
JAMES DUNN,
R. CRUIKSHANK,   Vestrymen,
JOHN SUTTON,

This was just after the Revolution against England and the American Declaration of Inde-pendence.

VESTRY UPHOLDS THE BISHOP'S AUTHORITY.

Nov. 23, 1816. Resolved, as the opinion of the Vestry, that whereas certain Ministers of the Protestant Episcopal Church in this State have protested against the authority of the Bishop of this State (Bishop Meade) and have declared that they never will acknowledge his authority as Bishop, that therefore the Vestry consider it incumbent on them to call upon their present Rector, Mr. Handy, to state explicitly whether he does acknowledge the authority of the Bishop of this State or not. In reply Mr. Handy unequivocally declared that he did not acknowledge the authority of the Bishop of this State; that he looked upon him as an usurper, and that he considered him only as a Presbyter in the Church.

Sunday, 24th Nov., 1816. Resolved, that the Vestry conceived it to be their duty, not from any personal objections against Mr. Handy, but as members of the Church acknowledging Her supreme authority, not to make any contract with The Rev. Mr. Handy for the ensuing year.

The Register, Mr. Robt. Dunn, to furnish the Rev. Mr. Handy and the Rev. Mr. Turner, one of the Standing Committee, with a copy of the foregoing proceedings.

.

.

SUBSCRIBERS TO RECTOR'S SALARY IN 1841.

Thomas Miller	$20 00		Sophia Neale	$10 00
Merritt Miller	20 00		James P. Gale	10 00
Joseph T. Mitchell	20 00		Doct. Browne	10 00
Dr. Ricaud	10 00		Wm. B. Willner	10 00
Joseph Harris	10 00		Ann Cruikshank	2 50
Hynson Smith	5 00		H. W. Carvill	10 00
Samuel Hodges	10 00		John P. Smith	2 00
Colin F. Hale	5 00		A. Roeder	1 00
Wm. W. Browne	5 00		George Roeder	1 50
Joseph N. Gordon, Jr.	5 00		John R. Stroud	5 00
Alexander W. Ringgold	20 00		Joseph Browne, 3d	5 00
James P. Wickes	20 00		L. Wickes	1 00
Wm. B. Everett	20 00		Basin M. Gale	5 00
Thos. R. Browne			J. Browne	10 00
Wm. Caten	2 00		G. D. S. Handy	1 00
Wm. Shaw	2 00		T. M. Blackiston	5 00
John Urie	10 00		Richard Smyth	2 00
Thos. P. Gresham	1 00		Thomas Lusby	3 00
John S. Constable	2 00		William Wickes	5 00
H. Beck	10 00			
	$197 00			$101 50
				197 00
				$298 50

SUBSCRIBERS TO PEWS FOR REPAIRING ST PAUL'S CHURCH.

March 15, 1841.

Judge E. F. Chambers, Chestertown	$20 00
Judge Jno. B. Ecclestown "	20 00
Col. Joseph Wickes, "	20 00
Mr. George S. Hollyday, "	20 00
Dr. Joseph N. Gordon (Co. cl'k), Chestertown	20 00
Mr. Rich'd S. Thomas, Chesterton.	20 00
James Boon, Georgetown, Md	20 00
Henry W. Carvill, Kent Co	20 00
Robert A. Gamble, Kent Co.	20 00
James Browne, near Chestertown	20 00
Capt'n Rich'd Smyth, near Chestertown	20 00
Mr. John R. Stroud " "	20 00
Thomas Blackiston, " "	10 00
M. Dillehunt and G. Hines, near Chestertown	20 00
John C. Hynson, near Rock Hall, Md.	20 00
Dr. L. M. Ricaud, " . " "	20 00
Mr. Tho's Miller " "	20 00
Alex'r W. Ringgold, near " "	20 00
James P. Wickes, Eastern Neck Island	20 00
Horatio Beck, Broad Knox (See Note, page 3)	20 00
Capt'n Merritt Miller, Swan Creek	20 00
The Misses Harris, Rock Hall	20 00
Mr. Wm. B. Everett, near Rock Hall	20 00
Wm. B. Wilmer, Belair	20 00
Mrs. Sophia Neale, Broad Neck	20 00
Mr. James F. Browne, near Chestertown	20 00
James P. Gale, Broad Neck	20 00
Mrs. E. Everett, Fairley Neck	21 00
March 15, 1841.—Total Subscriptions to pews	$550 00
June 2, 1841. Net Proceeds of Fair at St. Paul's Church	650 00
1841. Subscriptions to Rector's Salary	298 50
Money raised by St. Paul's in 1841	$1498 50

LAWRENCE M. RICAUD, Register.

1841.—Cost of Repairs in 1841 was	$1625 54

CHANCEL.

Plan of Pews as Allotted to Subscribers in the Church of St.
Paul's in 1842.

This Plan is as per Copy in Record Book No. 2.

CHURCH 40x30.

There is no No. 25 Pew
and the plan is for
48 Pews.

44 Joseph Wickes.		45 Dr. Ricaud.	1 Henry Carvill.	2 John R. Stroud.
42 R. S. Thomas.		43 Wm. B. Wilmer	3 James P. Gale.	4 James Boon.
40 Geo. Hollyday.		41 Jno. C. Hynson.	5 Jas. H. Browne	6. E. F. Chambers
38 J. B. Eccleston.		39 Thos. Miller.	7 Horatio Beck.	8 Mrs. S. Neale.
36 Stove.		37 Gordon Ricaud	9	10 Stove.
34 Open Seat.		35 Gordon.	11 Merritt Miller.	12 Open Seat.
32 R. A. Gamble.		33 James Browne	13 Mrs. H. Everett	14
30 M. Dillehunt.		31 Rich'd Smyth.	15 A. W. Ringgold	16
28 Jas. P. Wickes		29	17	18
26 Brown.		27	19	20
24 Mrs. E. Everett.				21
23				22

AISLES 3 FEET WIDE; PEWS 2 FEET 8 INCHES APART. (HOUSE OF PEWS DRAWN FOR BY LOT, ON JULY 23RD, 1842.

Stairway
to Gallery.

Door.

APPENDIX II.

LAND DEEDS.

1897, May 16. ENTERED BY LAWRENCE M. RICAUD, Reg'r.

The Rev'd Sam'l Gordon sent me a list of papers concerning St. Paul's Church:

No. 1.—Deed from Mackey to Thomas Ringgold, 1750, recorded in the Land Records of Kent county, Liber I. S. No. 2, folio 451, 11 acres, Mackey's Desire, and part of Arcadia.

No. 2. Deed from Thomas Ringgold to James Dunn, dated 21st Jany. 1751, Liber I. S. No 27, folio 385, 2½ acres.

No. 3. Deed from Thomas Ringgold to William Dunn, dated March 2d, 1761 (by estimation 17½ acres).

No. 4. Deed from Thomas Ringgold to Ralph Page, Wm. Ringgold, James Frisby, James Dunn, Charles Hynson and Benjamin Ricaud, gentlemen, and Vestrymen of St. Paul's Parish. Five acres, a Gift—1767.

True Copy—Test: LAWRENCE M. RICAUD, REGISTER.

MR. GEORGE BECK'S LIST OF SUBSCRIBERS TO THE CEMETERY FENCE IN 1890—1.

Chas. T. Westcott	$25 00	Mrs. Wm. Tomlinson	1 00
R. D. Hynson	25 00	Misses Bell	30 00
Anna M. Westcott	25 00	Wm Ford	5 00
Dr. Sam'l Beck	25 00	John Brice	5 00
Josias Ringgold	25 00	Mrs Celena Jessop	5 00
Sarah A. Handy	20 00	Wm. H. Jones	2 00
Spencer Harris	10 00	Charles T. Stratton	2 00
T. Rouie Strong	10 00	Miss Clothier	5 00
Geo. Z. Greenwood	10 00	H. Clay Usilton	2 50
Alex'r Harris	10 00	S. C. Lecompt	5 00
James Hodges	20 00	J. Walter Skirven	10 00
William S. Walker	10 00	Thomas Blackiston	2 00
B. F. Beck, Sr	10 00	R. S. Jones	2 00
Mrs. A. Willmer	10 00	C. B. Beck	50
Mrs. C. V. Newman	5 00	Mrs. A. Strong	5 00
Per. Mrs. Kate Gordon	122 31	Mrs. James A. Merritt	10 00
P. Willmer	5 00	Mrs. Louisa Thomas	5 00
H. S. Francis	1 00	Samuel Lee	1 00
G. H. Dutton	10 00	H. H. Barroll	5 00
Wm. French	1 00	Miss Mollie Allen	1 00
J. W. Beachamp	1 00	Wash'n Skirven	12 00
J. P. Nicholson	1 50	I. C. Taylor	6 00
W. B. Willmer	2 00	Rev. Dr. J. A. Eccleston	25 00
Mrs. Houston	5 00	V. B. Hines	5 00
Dr. S. T. Earle	5 00	L. C. Ayres	2 00
John Jones	1 00	Joseph Rasin	5 00
Mrs. Thomas Hill	25 00	Geo. B. Westcott	2 00
Charles Brown	1 00	V. Hendrickson	1 00
Robt. Hatcherson	2 00	Charles Wickes	1 00
Nathan Crow	1 00	John Bordley	1 00
J. H. Gale	8 00	Pere Hague	15 00
T. W. Skirven	6 00	W. A. Hyland	5 00
Mrs. Isaac Rogers	1 00	Robt. Hodges	25 00
Mrs. McClintock	5 00		
J. E. Gilpin	5 00		$666 81

CHURCH OFFICERS, 1882 to 1893.

SENIOR WARDEN.
Geo. A. Jessop, - for 12 years.

JUNIOR WARDENS.
Thomas Ringgold, - - for 1 year.
Harry Nicols, - - - for 5 years.
Israel F. Walbert, - " 3 "
J. Thos. Blackiston, - - " 2 "

VESTRYMEN.
Josias Ringgold, - for 1 year.
Joseph Rasin, - for 12 years.
George Beck, - - " 11 "
George Bell, - - " 11 "
S. Constable, - - " 12 "
J. C. Wheatley, - - " 9 "
T. A. Hulme, - - for 5 years.

James Rankin, - for 8 years.
Mr. Thompson, " 1 "
R. I. Taylor, " 6 "
Walter B. Strong, - " 7 "
L. R. Shewell, " 1 "
R. Sterling Jones - - " 2 "
I. F. Walbert, - - " 2 "
Thos. W. Skirven, - - " 2 "

TREASURER.
George Beck, - - for 7 years.

REGISTRARS.
Stevenson Constable - for 12 years.
L. R. Shewell, - - " 1 "

COLLECTOR.
I. F. Walbert, - - for 1 year.

OFFICERS IN 1893.

Rector—Chris. T. Denroche. Lay Reader—L. R. Shewell.
Wardens—George A. Jessop and J. Thos. Blackiston.
Vestry Joseph Rasin, George Bell, George Beck, Walter B. Strong, L. R. Shewell.
I. F. Walbert, R. Sterling Jones, Thos. W. Skirven.
Delegate to Convention—George Bell; alternate, George Beck.
Treasurer—George Beck.
Registrar—Linington Roberts Shewell.
Collector— Israel F. Walbert.
Superintendent of Cemetery—Thomas W. Skirven.
Director of Music—Mrs. Thomas W. Skirven.
Organist Miss Lizzie Corey.
Sunday School Superintendent—Mrs. Thomas W. Skirven.
Sexton—Joseph Mensch.
Parish Horse—" Bob," well worthy of honorable mention.

FESTIVALS.

MANAGED BY THE VESTRY, ASSISTED BY THE LADIES AID AND SEWING SOCIETY.

1841, 25th June; net $650.00.
1885, 25th Sept.; net, $112.46. Expenses, $101.85 ; Total, $214.31.
1886, 5th July ; net, $37.18.
1887, 14th March ; net, $43.35.
1887, 19th Sept.; net, $169.54.
1889, 8th Sept.; net, $122.10.
1890, 22d Sept.; net, $130.98.
1898, 16th Sept.; net, $131.00.
1892, June ; net, $87.00. Expenses, $37.32 ; Total, $124.32.
1892, Sept.: net, $84.16.

HOUSE RENTED IN FAIRLEE VILLAGE.

1887, 19th Sept. The Vestry decided to Rent the Glebe and the Glebe House to a Tenant, and to Rent a house elsewhere for the Rector.

1888, 3d April. Mr. George Bell, as a committee of Vestry, rented the "Skirven" House for a Rectory, at $77.91, and the Kendall stable for $8.0 .

1888, 27th Sept. The Vestry Rented the "Meeks'" House at $125.00; I. U. to pay one-third of the Rent; the Rent of the Glebe to meet the Balance.

1893. The "Meeks'" house property and lot is still used as the Rector's dwelling.

BI CENTENNIAL CELEBRATION IN 1893.

CELEBRATION OF THE 200TH ANNIVERSARY OF THE FOUNDATION OF ST. PAUL'S PARISH, ON MAY 24TH AND 25TH, 1893.

The Celebration was proposed by Mr. Stevenson Constable, then the Registrar, but now deceased.

It was held in St. Paul's Church, and on the Church grounds. The Invited Guests were the 6 ex-Rectors.

1. The Rev'd Edward H. C. Goodwin, Governor's Island, N. Y.
2. The Rev'd Robert Willson, Charleston, S. C.
3. The Rev'd S. S. Hepburn, Old Church, Hanover county, Va.
4. The Rev'd William Munford, Salisbury, Wicomico county, Md.
5.—The Rev'd George C. Sutton, Shrewsbury Parish, Kent county, Md.
6.—The Rev'd S. C. Roberts, of Emmanuel Church, Chestertown, Kent county, Md., at intervals a pro. tem. Rector of St. Paul's Church.

The Rt. Rev'd William Forbes Adams, D. D., Bishop of the Diocese of Easton in the State of Maryland.

The Rt. Rev'd William Paret, D. D., Bishop of the Diocese of Maryland.

The Rev'd George Stokes, Govanstown, Md.

The Rev'd J. Houston Eccleston, D. D., Baltimore Md.

Rev'd John Martin, Port Deposit, Md.

Rev'd Henry B. Martin, Princess Anne, Md.

Rev. Algernon Batte, Church Hill, Md.

The Rev'd H. C. E. Costelle, Sharpsburg, Maryland.

The Rev. Peregrine Wroth, Baltimore, Md.

The Members of the Northern Convocation of the Diocese of Easton.

James A. Pearce, Esq., Chancellor of the Diocese of Easton, Chestertown, Md.

Charles T. Westcott, Esq., Chestertown, Md.

R. C. Mackall, M. D., Elkton, Cecil county, Md.

Members of the Maryland Historical Society, Baltimore, Md., and the Congregation of Christ Church, I. U.

THE REV. CHRIS. T. DENROCHE,

--RECTOR OF

St. Paul's Church, Kent County, Md., and of Christ Church, in I. U. District, Kent county, Md.

ERRATA.

PAGE 3: In note at foot, "appendix E." should be appendix F.

ON PAGE 18: after the Rev. Mr. Bordley's appointment, SEE that of the Rev. Alex. Williamson, on page 8.

PAGE 21: for two entries on Cemetery SEE page 13 on dates Jan. 10, 1845 and Nov. 19, 1845.

PAGE 22: Gearge D. S. Handy, should be George D. S. Handy.

PAGE 22: 1890, 22nd September, SEE appendix H page 40.

PAGE 25: Mr. Hagee should be Mr. Hague.

PAGE 25: "Memorials"; for that of Mr. and Mrs. George Beck's children, SEE page 16, at July 22nd. 1882.

PAGE 28: L. M. Ricand 1879, should be 1869.

ON PAGE 40: after "Mr. George Beck's list of subscribers to the Cemetery fence in 1890–1", SEE the last two paragraphs on page 22, dated 1890, 22nd September.

INDEX TO BOOK.

INDEX TO APPENDIX.

www.ingramcontent.com/pod-product-compliance
Lightning Source LLC
Chambersburg PA
CBHW030903260626
47169CB00008B/2669

* 9 7 8 3 3 3 7 4 2 9 4 9 2 *